Hava, Poofy and the Magical Firewood

Published by Amped Journey, Inc.

ISBN-13:

Paperback: 979-8-9909642-0-4
Hardback: 979-8-9909642-1-1
eBook: 979-8-9909642-2-8

Published by:
Amped Journey, Inc. 13 Summit Square Center, Unit 226, Langhorne, Pennsylvania 19047

Library of Congress Cataloging-in-Publication Data

Printed in the United States of America and Europe

First Edition

For Hava, who inspired us to go after our dreams,
for Poofy, who inspired us to embrace our fears,
and for the many friends, family, and others who have
helped us in so many ways on this magical journey to
creating this book.

A huge thanks to Gramps, Nana Bonbon, Buni, Grandma,
and Andrei for your incredible support in making our
Dream Supernova Big project a success!

And a special thanks to Laura whose creative vision and
wizardry brought a whole new level of magic to our story.

Sea of Special Souls
VILLAGE

Cave of Whispers
Mountain of Miracles
Meadow of Dreams

Once there was a girl named Hava who had a big heart, a kind soul, and a beautiful spirit.

Hava was very brave, loved to be silly and sweet, and she loved to paint with watercolors.

One day, Hava was painting when she felt the air inside suddenly get cold.

She went to ask her mom about it.

GR
BLUE

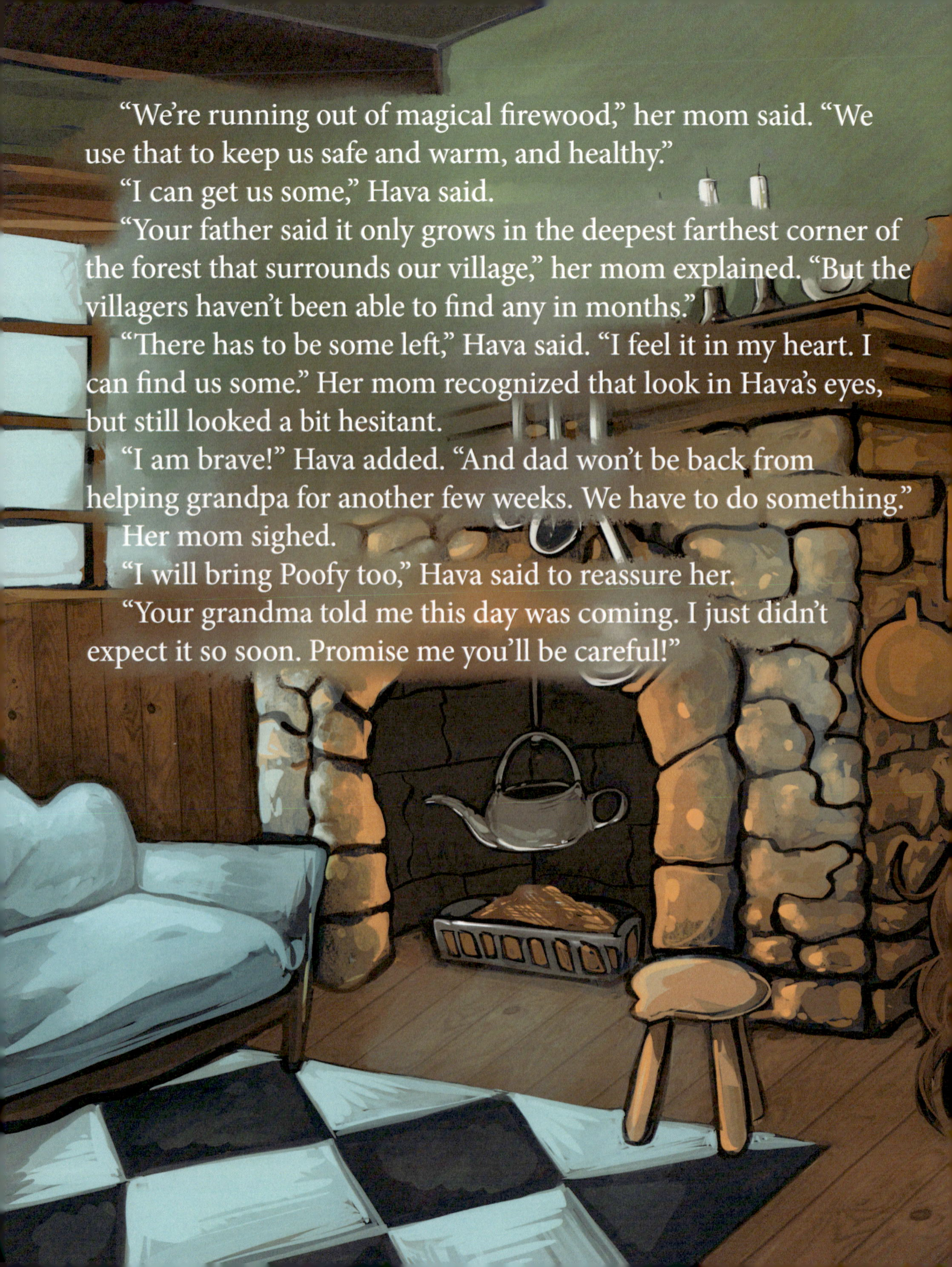

“We’re running out of magical firewood,” her mom said. “We use that to keep us safe and warm, and healthy.”

“I can get us some,” Hava said.

“Your father said it only grows in the deepest farthest corner of the forest that surrounds our village,” her mom explained. “But the villagers haven’t been able to find any in months.”

“There has to be some left,” Hava said. “I feel it in my heart. I can find us some.” Her mom recognized that look in Hava’s eyes, but still looked a bit hesitant.

“I am brave!” Hava added. “And dad won’t be back from helping grandpa for another few weeks. We have to do something.”

Her mom sighed.

“I will bring Poofy too,” Hava said to reassure her.

“Your grandma told me this day was coming. I just didn’t expect it so soon. Promise me you’ll be careful!”

Hava hugged her mom and rushed outside to her best friend's house next door. Poofy and Hava had been best friends for as long as either could remember. Poofy was just like Hava. She also had a big heart, a kind soul, and a beautiful spirit. But unlike Hava, she was a zebra, and she was scared of many things. Hava told her about the magical firewood.

Poofy hesitated, "I don't know Hava, that sounds really scary."

"I'm scared too," Hava said. "But together we can be brave and scared at the same time. I wouldn't ask unless it was really important."

Poofy didn't want to let her friend down, so she agreed to go. And off they went out of the village into the forest.

As they walked deeper and deeper into the forest, the sun gave way to clouds, and the clouds gave way to darker clouds, and the darker clouds gave way to rain, and the rain gave way to thunder, and the thunder gave way to lightning.

No matter how fast Hava and Poofy ran, no matter which diretion they went, the storm continued.

Poofy looked up to the clouds all cold and wet.

"I wish we could fly above the clouds, then we wouldn't have to stay down here in this rain."

That reminded Hava of a story her grandmother used to tell her of a special zebra that could fly. She told Poofy about it.

Poofy started laughing, "A zebra...that can fly? Please, that's just silly. Zebras can't fly!"

"But have you ever tried to fly?" Hava asked.

"No, why would I do that? I walk and run on the ground!"

"Then how do you know you can't fly?" Hava said. "I believe in you Poofy. And I'll be right here beside you. What do you have to lose?"

Poofy looked up anxiously.
“What if I can’t?” she whispered.
“What if you can?” Hava asked bravely.

Poofy began to run...faster and faster. When she couldn't go any faster she pushed with all her might and she went up into the air a little bit.

Just as she thought she was going to come back down to the ground, she pushed and kicked again with all her strength, and she went higher and higher and higher, until she realized she was actually flying.

"Oh my god I am flying. Woohooo! Oh yeah, this Zebra here can fly. I can really fly!" Poofy said exhilarated.

Hava laughed and yelled up, "See I knew you could fly. I just knew you could!"

"Thank you so much for believing in me," Poofy said, as she came back down to the ground. "I never ever would have tried to fly if it weren't for you. Now let's get out of this rain."

Hava jumped on Poofy's back and together they flew up beyond the clouds. The sun popped back out and they dried off as they flew straight to the deepest farthest corner of the forest that surrounds their village.

When they landed, they couldn't believe what they saw. Trees of majestic size stood over them, letting in streams of light that revealed every tree was covered with a kind of thick, dark grime.

The trees looked very weak and at the base of each one were piles of trash that must have been left there from other villagers. Hava looked around every tree, trying to find even one piece of magical firewood.

But none was to be found.

"The trees look sad," Poofy observed.

"I thought this place was supposed to be magical."

Hava stopped by one of the smaller trees. She anxiously ran her fingers along one of the branches until she suddenly saw a star shape carved gently into the side of it.

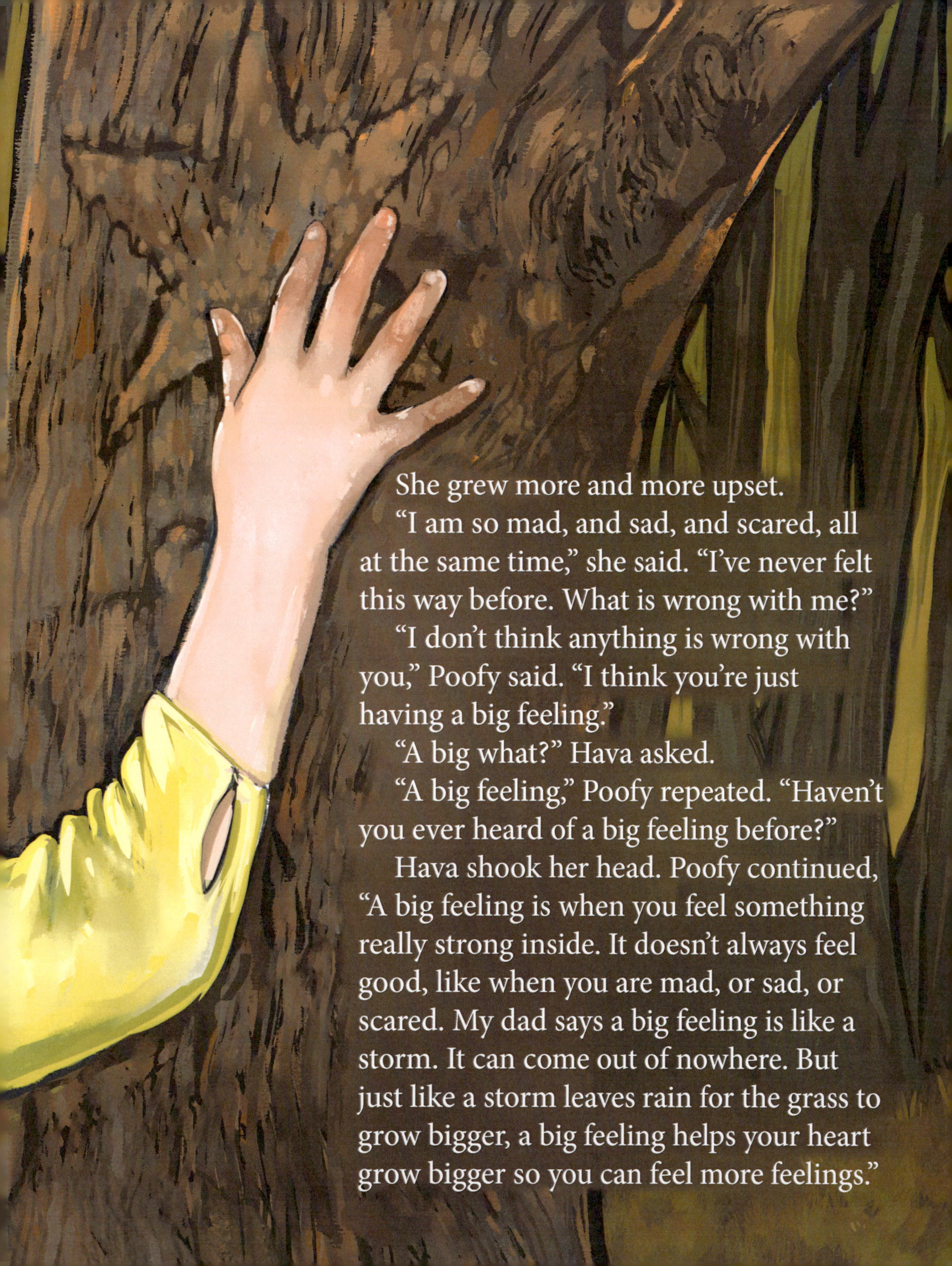

She grew more and more upset.

"I am so mad, and sad, and scared, all at the same time," she said. "I've never felt this way before. What is wrong with me?"

"I don't think anything is wrong with you," Poofy said. "I think you're just having a big feeling."

"A big what?" Hava asked.

"A big feeling," Poofy repeated. "Haven't you ever heard of a big feeling before?"

Hava shook her head. Poofy continued, "A big feeling is when you feel something really strong inside. It doesn't always feel good, like when you are mad, or sad, or scared. My dad says a big feeling is like a storm. It can come out of nowhere. But just like a storm leaves rain for the grass to grow bigger, a big feeling helps your heart grow bigger so you can feel more feelings."

Hava leaned against the tree and closed her eyes.

"I'm scared," she whispered. "I don't know if I can do this."

"It's scary," Poofy said. "But my dad also says there is nothing more brave than someone who can feel a big feeling. I believe in you Hava. I'll be right here beside you."

Hava started to cry. Poofy stepped a bit closer and placed a loving hand on Hava's shoulder. The two best friends stood there in the deepest farthest corner of the forest as the big feeling grew stronger and stronger inside of Hava.

Just as she thought she couldn't take anymore, a few tears fell from Hava's eye.

They landed on the center of the star that was carved in the branch. It started to glow subtly, but neither of the two friends noticed.

Hava then felt the wave of big feelings pass. She wiped her eyes and smiled at Poofy.

"Thank you Poofy. My heart does feel bigger. But can we go home now?"

Poofy nodded and knelt down. As Hava was about to hop on her back, she noticed the star shape glowing brighter along with the rest of the tree. It no longer had any dark grime on it.

"It's the magical firewood," Hava yelled out. "It glows just like my grandma told me in her stories!"

"Wow," Poofy said. "Now that's what I call magical! But aren't we going to need a lot more than this? The whole village needs some."

"A tiny piece of magical firewood lasts a long time," Hava explained. "But my grandma said the most important thing is to always leave some behind otherwise more can't grow."

From that one branch, they collected enough magical firewood to share with the whole village. Before leaving, Hava gave the tree a big hug.

"Thank you," she said.

Together Hava and Poofy flew back into the sky. As they got closer to the village, the people stared up at them in wonder and started to cheer.

As they landed in the middle of the crowd, Hava saw her mom nearby. She ran up to her and gave her the biggest hug.

"I'm so proud of you for being so brave and getting the magical firewood," her mom said.

"I was even braver than that!"

"How so?" her mom asked.

"I felt a big feeling!"

"A big what?"

Hava smiled. "I'll tell you all about it later. Let's go celebrate!"

For the rest of the night, the whole town sang and ate and danced in front of magical fires built with magical firewood.

Ava & David Lederman -Authors

Ava & David are a father-daughter duo who love creating, telling, and listening to stories that spark the imagination and speak to the soul. They came up with the first Hava and Poofy story when Ava was three. They quickly found Hava and Poofy and the adventures they unfolded were powerful tools to help Ava navigate the transition from being a toddler to becoming a "big kiddo." One book turned into five and they are currently working on the 6th story in the series. Ava is a force of life who loves ice cream, Harry Potter, doing crafts and drawing, going on walks with her dog Qi, and tickle-fests with her dad. David loves being Ava's father, writing, being in nature, and inspiring people young and old to trust in themselves and embrace the adventures of life.

Laura Hammond
-Illustrator

Laura Hammond is an illustrator, event artist and caricaturist. Her vibrant artwork has not only been featured in publications such as Buzzfeed and The Huffington Post, but she has many published illustrated works. From children's books and comics to logo designs and caricature portraits, she's done it all. She has also designed sets for the theaters in her hometown of Muskogee, Oklahoma. In her free time, she's busy watching movies with her extremely handsome husband Matthew and her rediculously bratty dog, Ivory. Laura is a regularly featured caricature artist at Oklahoma Soonercon, Oktoberfest, Tulsa Art Crawls, and pop-up events around the state. You can find more of her work at LauraDrawsMe.com

Hava started to tear up. She loved her dad more than anything in the world.

"He needs a miracle," the village doctor continued.

That reminded Hava of a story her grandmother used to tell her of a special mountain, called the Mountain of Miracles, which stood beyond the forest that surrounds their village. Legend said if you could find the disappearing raindrops that fell on that mountain you would find the power to heal. But the mountain was nearly impossible to climb and no one in the village had ever done so.

Even though Hava was very scared, she knew what she had to do. She wiped away her tears, took a deep breath, grabbed her coat, and ran outside to find Poofy.

Many More Adventures to Come

Be sure to collect all the books coming soon in the series:

Hava, Poofy and the Magical Firewood

Hava, Poofy and the Mountain of Miracles

Hava, Poofy and the Treasure of Goo

Hava, Poofy and the Island that Sinks

Hava, Poofy and the Cave of Whispers

Hava, Poofy and the Volcano of Tears

Milton Keynes UK
Ingram Content Group UK Ltd.
UKRC030844210924
448499UK00005B/15

HORSES AND OTHER ANIMALS IN MOTION

45 CLASSIC PHOTOGRAPHIC SEQUENCES

EADWEARD MUYBRIDGE

DOVER PUBLICATIONS, INC.
NEW YORK

This Dover edition, first published in 1985, is a selection of 45 sequences from the eleven-volume work *Animal Locomotion: an electro-photographic investigation of consecutive phases of animal movements*, originally published under the auspices of the University of Pennsylvania, Philadelphia, in 1887. A publisher's note (adapted from that for *The Male and Female Figure in Motion: 60 Classic Photographic Sequences*; Dover 24745-7), captions and contents have been prepared especially for this edition. The publisher's note draws heavily upon Anita Ventura Mozley's introduction to the Dover edition of the complete work, entitled *Muybridge's Complete Human and Animal Locomotion* (three vols.: 23792-3; 23793-1; 23794-X).

DOVER *Pictorial Archive* SERIES

Manufactured in the United States of America
Dover Publications, Inc., 31 East 2nd Street, Mineola, N.Y. 11501

Library of Congress Cataloging in Publication Data

Muybridge, Eadweard, 1830–1904.
Horses and other animals in motion.

"A selection of 45 sequences from the eleven-volume Animal locomotion, an electro-photographic investigation of consecutive phases of animal movements, originally published under the auspices of the University of Pennsylvania, Philadelphia, in 1887"—

1. Animal locomotion—Pictorial works. I. Title.
QP301.M846 1985 599'.01852 85-6752
ISBN 0-486-24911-5 (pbk.)